Why the Leopard Has Spots

Retold by Katherine Mead
Illustrated by Barry Rockwell

STECK-VAUGHN
COMPANY
ELEMENTARY • SECONDARY • ADULT • LIBRARY

Contents

The Most Beautiful Leopard

Once upon a time, in a jungle village far, far away, a beautiful leopard cub was born. His mother and father were so proud and happy that they named him Momuli-Bintu-Sakee. That means "Most Beautiful Baby in the World." They called him Momu.

In those days, leopards were just one
color all over. They were a beautiful
brown-yellow. No stripes, no spots, and
no patches covered their bodies. Momu
was the most beautiful of all. He looked
golden in the sunlight.

"We are so lucky to have him," said
his parents. They loved to show him off.

4

All the animals agreed that Momu
was beautiful. Even Cheetah said so.
  "He is the most beautiful leopard,
but I am still the most beautiful animal
in the whole jungle," said Cheetah. The
other animals often stopped to admire
Momu's beautiful golden coat.

Momu Grows Up

As Momu grew, he became more and more handsome and friendly and kind. He always said "please" and "thank you." All the animals in the village liked him.

The animal mothers often said to their babies, "Go play with Momu. He's such a nice leopard."

Momu was not perfect. He wasn't very neat. As hard as he tried, Momu just couldn't do anything neatly. Each time he ate, food was all over the table, the floor, and worst of all, all over Momu!

Momu's mother tried her best to teach him to be neat. "Take little bites of food, dear," said his mother. So Momu took little bites.

"Try not to get so dirty," said his father. So Momu tried, but it still didn't make him neat.

Poor Momu was still messy. He took even smaller bites.

He tried not to get dirty, but nothing seemed to help.

His mother scrubbed and rubbed Momu to keep him clean. "Someday you'll learn to be neat, Momu," said his mother.

Each day Momu tried again.

Momu kept getting more and more
messy. One day his friend Elephant
thought it would be fun to play in the
mud at the watering hole. So did Momu.
Soon they were covered in mud from
their heads to their toes. What a mess!

At the end of the day, Elephant went
for a long, long swim. Elephant liked
the water. Momu didn't like the water.

When Elephant came out of the water,
she was very clean and very wrinkled.
Momu went home just as he was.

When he got in the house, Momu tracked mud on the floor. He tracked mud on the chairs. There was mud everywhere. Momu's mother frowned at him. "Oh, Momu," she said. "Will you ever learn to be neat?"

"I'll try," said Momu.

Momu's mother rubbed and scrubbed to get him clean. His father mopped and washed the floor. They all cleaned the chairs. Then they kissed their beautiful clean son and put him to bed.

"Tomorrow, I'll be neat," said Momu.

"We know you'll try," said his parents.

The next day, Momu and Lion went to the woods. They stopped to rest under a gumberry tree. Gumberries are big and red. They are full of sticky, gummy juice.

Lion and Momu started tossing berries. Soon Momu was sticky and gummy. So was Lion.

They laughed at themselves. They were two messy friends.

"What a mess," said Momu.

"I'd better clean up," said Lion. So Lion sat down and licked himself clean.

Momu ran home just as he was.

Momu ran in the house. He tracked sticky, gummy juice on the floor. He tracked sticky, gummy juice on the chairs. Sticky, gummy red juice was everywhere.

"Oh, Momu," said his father. "Will you ever learn to be neat?"

"I'll try," said Momu.

Momu's father rubbed and scrubbed
to get him clean. His mother mopped
and washed the floor. They all cleaned
the chairs. Then they kissed their clean
son and put him to bed.

"Tomorrow, I'll be neat," said Momu.

"We know you'll try," said his parents.

Momu's Plan

Momu was tired of being messy. But
as hard as he tried, he just couldn't be
neat. His room was a mess. Everything
he owned was a mess! What could he do
to prove he could be neat?

The next morning, Momu sat under a tree thinking. There had to be a way to show everyone that he could be neat.

Momu stared at their house. The paint was dull and old. It needed new paint. Momu smiled. He had a plan!

That very day, Momu's mother and father were going out to hunt for food. Momu would have the house to himself.

Before they left, Momu's mother said, "Please, darling one, promise me you won't get into anything messy while we are gone."

"I do promise," said Momu. "You'll see. I will be very neat."

"Well, good-bye. We'll be back home tonight," Father said. They kissed Momu and went off to the deep woods to hunt.

Momu watched them go. Then he ran out to the shed.

Momu's Surprise

Momu knew that his parents were always busy rubbing and scrubbing and mopping and washing him. They had no time to paint the house.

Momu would paint the house. He'd be very neat. He would be neater than he had ever been!

First, Momu had to decide on a color to paint the house. It had to be a special color. Momu remembered how he liked the dark brown stripes that his friend Tiger had.

"That's it!" said Momu. "I'll paint the house a lovely dark brown."

And so Momu was ready to paint … very neatly!

Momu took the pail of beautiful dark
brown paint. He found a big, wide brush.
   "This should be easy," thought Momu.
"I just have to be neat."
   Momu did not think that would be
hard. He would be very careful.

By the time the sun was high in the sky, Momu had painted the front of the house and all the doors. He was doing a good job.

"It's not so hard to be neat," thought Momu. He stopped and looked around. The ground was covered with paint. But Momu had only gotten a few drops of paint on himself.

"It's just a little paint. It will wash off," he thought. "I'm just learning to be neat, after all."

By afternoon, there was still a lot to paint. Momu had half the house to do. And it would soon be too dark to paint.

"I'd better hurry," Momu said to himself. But the more he hurried, the more he spilled. "It will wash off," he thought. "Soon I'll be very clean and neat again."

When the sun sank low in the sky, Momu finished. The house looked bright and new. It was a beautiful dark chocolate color.

After the last brush stroke, Momu sat down to admire his work. "It looks wonderful," said Momu. "I'll just wash off this mess." But he was so tired that he fell asleep.

When night fell, Momu's parents
came back home. They saw their house
in the moonlight.

"It's beautiful!" they said. "Who could
have done such a wonderful thing?"

"Well, whoever it was did a very neat
job!" said Father.

"Yes, I love the color," said Mother.
They ran to find Momu.

"Momu, where are you? Do you know who painted the house?" they asked.

"Here I am," said Momu. "I painted the house for you. I wanted to surprise you. I did a neat job."

"Yes, the house looks neat. And it looks like you painted yourself, too!" said his parents.

"Oh, Mother and Father," said Momu. "I fell asleep before I cleaned up. Now these spots won't come off!"

Momu's mother and father looked at their son. They saw the lovely pattern made by the brown spots on his body.

"Thank you for painting the house for us. Son, you are even more beautiful than before," they said. "We could hunt better in the jungle with spots. Tomorrow we will get some spots, too." They kissed their tired, spotted leopard son and put him to bed.

The next day, Momu's parents painted spots on themselves. Then Momu and his parents went for a walk in the jungle. The other leopards saw their spots and wanted some of their own. So Momu painted spots on the other leopards.

Soon the news spread all across the jungle and beyond. Everyone was talking about the beautiful spotted leopards.

Other leopards came from far away to get spots. There were too many spots for Momu to paint. So he lined up all the leopards. He filled the brush with paint and shook it. Then every leopard was covered with beautiful spots.

From that day to this, all leopards are covered with beautiful dark brown spots. And they are always very neat.